Acting Edition

I0741572

Deceived

based on the play *Gaslight*
by Patrick Hamilton

adapted by Johnna Wright
and Patty Jamieson

FOR PRODUCTION INQUIRIES
UNITED STATES AND CANADA
info@concordtheatricals.com
1-866-979-0447

UNITED KINGDOM AND EUROPE
licensing@concordtheatricals.co.uk
020-7054-7298

Each title is subject to availability from Concord Theatricals Corp., depending upon country of performance. Please be aware that *DECEIVED* may not be licensed by Concord Theatricals Corp. in your territory. Professional and amateur producers should contact the nearest Concord Theatricals Corp. office or licensing partner to verify availability.

No one shall make any changes in this title(s) for the purpose of production. No part of this book may be reproduced, stored in a retrieval system, scanned, uploaded, or transmitted in any form, by any means, now known or yet to be invented, including mechanical, electronic, digital, photocopying, recording, videotaping, or otherwise, without the prior written permission of the publisher. No one shall share this title(s), or any part of this title(s), through any social media or file hosting websites.

For all inquiries regarding motion picture, television, online/digital and other media rights, please contact Concord Theatricals Corp.

MUSIC AND THIRD-PARTY MATERIALS USE NOTE

Licensees are solely responsible for obtaining formal written permission from copyright owners to use copyrighted music and/or other copyrighted third-party materials (e.g. artworks, logos) in the performance of this play and are strongly cautioned to do so. If no such permission is obtained by the licensee, then the licensee must use only original music and materials that the licensee owns and controls. Licensees are solely responsible and liable for clearances of all third-party copyrighted materials, including without limitation music, and shall indemnify the copyright owners of the play(s) and their licensing agent, Concord Theatricals Corp., against any costs, expenses, losses and liabilities arising from the use of such copyrighted third-party materials by licensees. For music, please contact the appropriate music licensing authority in your territory for the rights to any incidental music.

IMPORTANT BILLING AND CREDIT REQUIREMENTS

If you have obtained performance rights to this title, please refer to your licensing agreement for important billing and credit requirements.

DECEIVED, based on Patrick Hamilton's *Gaslight*, premiered as *Gaslight* in 2022 at the Shaw Festival (Tim Carroll, Artistic Director) in Niagara-on-the-Lake, Ontario, Canada. The performance was directed by Kelli Fox, with set and costume design by Judith Bowden, lighting design by Kimberly Purtell, and sound design by Gilles Zolty. The production stage manager was Amy Jewell, and the assistant stage manager was Leigh McClymont. The cast was as follows:

BELLA	Julie Lumsden
ELIZABETH	Kate Hennig
JACK	André Morin
NANCY	Julia Course

CHARACTERS

BELLA – A young married woman, about 25, with possibly a nervous disposition. Bella loves and trusts her husband, and only begins to doubt his sincerity when circumstances force her to do so. As the story progresses, she must accept a new reality, and find a strength – and cunning – she didn't know she had.

JACK – Her husband, 35–40, debonair and charming. Jack is the most loving, sympathetic and supportive partner he could possibly be, or so it seems for most of the play.

ELIZABETH – The housekeeper, 50s–60s, hard of hearing. A lifetime "in service" has taught her to remain as dutiful and discreet as possible, and to keep her opinions to herself except in extreme circumstances.

NANCY – The young housemaid, her eye on the main chance. Smart and perceptive, she thinks she sees an opportunity to outsmart everyone.

SETTING

The sitting room of a middle class house in a square in London.

TIME

1901.

AUTHOR'S NOTES

Our goal with this adaptation is to reclaim the classic thriller by allowing the female "victim" to be her own rescuer.

It's important to the story that the ending is not played from the beginning. A number of characters are not what they seem, but that should not be apparent early on.

We want the dialogue to fit within the classic thriller genre, but it should also feel and sound natural. We do not imagine the story being told in a melodramatic tone.

ACT ONE

Scene One

(A London Victorian row house. There is a credenza with many drawers and cubbies. There is a desk. There is a sofa, and a lamp with beaded trim. We can see a hallway and a staircase.)

(Late afternoon. Big Ben strikes five in the distance. **BELLA** *checks the tea things, which are laid out.)*

BELLA. *(Calling.)* Elizabeth! Elizabeth! Can you bring the flowers?

*(***ELIZABETH*** enters carrying a vase of flowers.)*

ELIZABETH. I'm sorry ma'am. I didn't quite hear you.

BELLA. That's alright. I just wanted to make sure we had everything. Those are perfect.

ELIZABETH. Only from the back-garden ma'am, but they'll brighten things up.

BELLA. Jack will be home any moment. He'll be so surprised. Oh! I haven't had a thing to eat since breakfast. I'm famished.

ELIZABETH. Those muffins look nice.

BELLA. Elizabeth –

> *(She takes one of the muffins and gives half to* **ELIZABETH**.*)*

here...

ELIZABETH. Oh my!

BELLA. *(With her mouth full.)* Our secret!

> *(They laugh.)*

ELIZABETH. The master will wonder what the occasion is – the good tea things, and all this.

BELLA. I am feeling well, Elizabeth. It's a beautiful day. That's the occasion.

> *(She hears something outside.)*

Oh! There's Jack!

> *(They jump up and quickly finish their muffins, and* **ELIZABETH** *exits to get the tea. After a moment,* **JACK** *enters.)*

JACK. Hello Bella. What's all this?

BELLA. It's tea.

JACK. Well yes, but...

BELLA. No occasion. I just wanted to make it special.

JACK. Thank you, Bella. Very nice indeed.

ELIZABETH. *(Enters with tea.)* The tea, ma'am. Sir.

BELLA. Thank you Elizabeth. Just here beside the muffins.

JACK. Muffins? Where did these come from? Did Elizabeth...

BELLA. I bought them this afternoon.

> *(***ELIZABETH** *exits.)*

JACK. You bought them.

BELLA. Yes, the muffin man –

JACK. Did you...

BELLA. No. I didn't go out. He came to the door.

JACK. Well, you answered the door. That's a step.

BELLA. Yes.

JACK. You did that for me. It's very thoughtful. Thank you.

And what other excitement did you find today?

BELLA. I think you'll be proud of me. I did all of the mending and planned the next week's menus with Elizabeth – though I have to ask her what she found at the market – and I paid the coal bill.

JACK. Industrious!

BELLA. Jack. I really feel stronger. Maybe I just need to have more to do. It's true what they say about an "idle mind."

JACK. You know how much I care about you, don't you?

(**BELLA** *nods.)*

Good.

Aren't those your mother's pearls?

BELLA. Yes!

JACK. What made you put them on today?

BELLA. I don't know. I suppose I was just looking for some encouragement. I remember her wearing these when I was a little girl. I think they're one of my favorite things in the whole world.

JACK. What?!

BELLA. Well, besides you of course!

(*They laugh.)*

JACK. Do be careful with them, though, Bella.

BELLA. Of course. Thank you.

JACK. I wouldn't mention it except –

BELLA. I know. I know. But that was... I'll be careful.

JACK. Well, this is a beautiful tea Bella, and it sounds like you've been very busy all day and that has been a good thing too.

BELLA. Yes. I –

JACK. Will you give me the receipt for the grocer's bill? You've paid that as well?

BELLA. The –?

JACK. The grocer's bill. I gave it to you yesterday.

BELLA. Oh yes. Of course. It must be in my workbox.

JACK. We can't be late paying it. Our credit...

BELLA. Don't worry, I'll find it. Or – it isn't lost. It's in my workbox.

(They drink their tea.)

JACK. Those pearls really do look beautiful on you, Bella.

BELLA. Thank you, Jack. I love them. Even though...

JACK. Even though it's sad, you still want to remember her.

BELLA. Yes... Are you going out tonight, Jack? The weather seems quite threatening all of a sudden.

JACK. Bella, you know my work is unpredictable. Since that Danby painting has fallen through, we definitely need to find a buyer for the bronze figurines.

BELLA. But can't you –

JACK. Now, now. If I don't look after the business, the business doesn't look after us, does it?

BELLA. No.

JACK. What's wrong?

BELLA. Oh, you know. I don't like it here alone at night. I – there are – *(Stops herself.)*

JACK. There are what, my dear?

BELLA. Nothing – nothing. I feel lonely without you, that's all.

JACK. You won't be alone. You'll have Elizabeth, and Nancy.

BELLA. Nancy? I don't – who...?

JACK. Nancy. The new maid. Remember?

BELLA. Oh – do we really need...?

JACK. Yes. You remember, don't you? She's coming this afternoon.

BELLA. I'm sorry, I...

JACK. It's all right. She'll be here soon, and you can meet her.

BELLA. I don't know why I can't remember.

JACK. It doesn't matter.

BELLA. Yes, it does. It does. Why can't I...?

JACK. Don't worry, my dear. We must always...

> *(**JACK** trails off as he notices something on the wall. There is a lighter rectangle where it seems a picture once hung.)*

BELLA. What is – *(Her gaze follows his.)* Oh. Oh no.

> *(**JACK** sighs.)*

JACK. Bella.

BELLA. The picture! It's gone again. Who took it down? Why has it been taken down?

JACK. I think that only you can answer that, Bella. Why was it taken down before? *(With sad resignation.)* Will you please get it from wherever you have hidden it, and put it back on the wall?

BELLA. But I haven't hidden it. I didn't. Jack, I don't know where it is. I swear I didn't... It must be...

JACK. Someone else? But at the moment there are only two other people living here, myself and Elizabeth. Are you suggesting that I –

BELLA. No dear, no! But –

(As **JACK** *moves toward the bell.)* Not Elizabeth, no, please Jack, don't ring for her. It's not – Elizabeth wouldn't...

(**JACK** *stops, looks at her helplessly.)*

JACK. Then if not me, and not Elizabeth... Bella...

(**BELLA** *hangs her head.)*

(With the utmost compassion.) My dear. I wish I understood. You know I try.

(**BELLA** *nods miserably.)*

Have you any idea at all where the picture is.

BELLA. *(Very softly.)* I suppose it's behind the [cupboard].*

JACK. Would you like me to go and see?

BELLA. No. No. I'll do it.

(**BELLA** *walks slowly to the spot and looks.)*

Yes. It's here.

JACK. *(Sadly.)* Then you did know where it was.

BELLA. No – no. I only guessed it was, because it was found there before.

---

* Or other suitable spot onstage.

JACK. It –

BELLA. It was found there twice before, yes, but I don't – I didn't...

JACK. *(Gently.)* Let's make this right, shall we? Shall I help you?

BELLA. No. I'll do it.

> (**BELLA** *removes the picture from its hiding spot. With great shame, she crosses to the wall and hangs it as* **JACK** *watches. It is a fairly large portrait of an attractive, vibrant woman in evening wear. She wears a stunning necklace of rubies.)*

JACK. Well done. Thank you.

BELLA. *(Softly.)* I didn't... I don't remember...

JACK. It's all right, Bella. Maybe this afternoon has been too much. Why don't you go lie down. You can meet Nancy later.

BELLA. Nancy...

JACK. *(Eternally patient.)* The new maid, my dear.

BELLA. Yes... Yes, you said that. All right.

> (**BELLA** *slowly climbs the stairs.* **JACK** *watches her go.)*

> (**ELIZABETH** *enters.)*

ELIZABETH. Pardon me, sir. I'm sorry to interrupt. *(She looks around, then quietly:)* Is Mrs. –?

JACK. She's gone upstairs to rest.

ELIZABETH. Oh. Is she all right?

JACK. Just a little tired.

ELIZABETH. I see.

(An unspoken acknowledgement.)

JACK. *(Glancing at the stairs to make sure* **BELLA** *is gone.)* Tell me something. Does she seem any better to you, these last few weeks?

ELIZABETH. *(Also checking the stairs.)* She seemed well enough this afternoon, sir.

JACK. Yes. I thought so too, but...

ELIZABETH. *(Hesitantly.)* Not anymore?

JACK. She said she felt very well, but in fact, she had...

> *(His eyes stray to the wall where the portrait now hangs.)*

ELIZABETH. Oh dear.

JACK. You hadn't taken it down, had you? To dust, or...

> (**ELIZABETH** *shakes her head.*)

ELIZABETH. Why does she do it, sir? Why would she take things in her own house, and hide them, and move them about?

JACK. I don't know.

It's very important that we continue to be kind and gentle with Mrs. Manningham, and to not bother her with everyday worries and problems.

ELIZABETH. Of course.

JACK. She needs rest, and calm. Until she's stronger, she needs to be protected a bit. Relieved of responsibility.

ELIZABETH. Sir. Might it be better to –

JACK. You've been wonderful to her for the past six months. You've shielded her. Can you...

ELIZABETH. Yes. Yes, sir.

JACK. Thank you. For the present, if she behaves strangely, or seems forgetful, let's reassure her. Do you understand?

ELIZABETH. Of course.

JACK. And, as always, if you notice anything – any change, or activity, that I should be aware of...

ELIZABETH. Yes, sir. I know my duty, sir.

JACK. Thank you. For her own protection. I don't know what else we can do for her.

ELIZABETH. *(Hopefully.)* Perhaps she just needs a bit more time to get accustomed to living here. It's not everyone that can live in a house where... *(Refers to the painting.)*

JACK. That's true. But Bella loves it here, in spite of that story. We both do.

(The doorbell rings.)

ELIZABETH. That'll be the new girl.

JACK. Yes. Show her in, please.

*(**ELIZABETH** exits. **JACK** stares at the painting.)*

*(**ELIZABETH** enters with **NANCY**.)*

ELIZABETH. Mr. Manningham. Nancy, say hello to the master.

*(**NANCY** curtsies somewhat carelessly.)*

NANCY. Sir.

JACK. Good afternoon, Nancy. Welcome to our home.

NANCY. Thank you, sir.

JACK. Elizabeth will show you your room, just down the hallway here. Mrs. Manningham is resting at present, but Elizabeth can show you around to start with.

NANCY. Yes, sir.

ELIZABETH. Oh, sir, I meant to tell you, I've had to put Nancy upstairs, at the back.

JACK. Upstairs! But I told you...

ELIZABETH. Yes, sir. But down here there was a problem with the window and the plaster's all gone to damp. It'll have to be replaced.

JACK. I see. But can't she...

ELIZABETH. I'm sorry, sir. I didn't know until I went in there yesterday. I should have...

JACK. No, you're right. I thought it would be more convenient for Nancy to be down here, but... Oh well! Off you go.

NANCY. Yes, sir.

ELIZABETH. This way.

(**ELIZABETH** *hustles* **NANCY** *out to the hall.*)

(**JACK** *gets a coat and scarf and exits.*)

Scene Two

*(Late morning. **ELIZABETH** surveys the room, then rings the bell. She rings it again. **NANCY** enters. She now wears a maid's uniform.)*

NANCY. Oh. It's only you. Why should I come when *you* ring the bell?

ELIZABETH. You come when the bell rings regardless of who rings it. You can clear these flowers away.

NANCY. Why couldn't you do it, you were already here.

ELIZABETH. If you like your position, missy, you'll take a more respectful tone.

NANCY. And who are you? *You* can't sack me, and the master won't.

ELIZABETH. Nancy. You'll learn to mind your manners, or you may wish you were dismissed.

*(**NANCY** takes the flowers away. **ELIZABETH** attends to the fire. She moves to tidy Jack's desk just as **JACK** enters the room.)*

JACK. Elizabeth!

ELIZABETH. Yes sir! Oh, you startled me!

JACK. What are you doing?

ELIZABETH. Nothing, sir. Just tidying.

JACK. Well, there's no need to tidy my desk. It's already in order – though it may not look that way!

ELIZABETH. Of course.

(She begins to leave the room.)

JACK. Where is Mrs. Manningham?

ELIZABETH. She's taking a short rest, sir.

JACK. Is she alright?

ELIZABETH. Yes, just a bit tired, she said.

JACK. Elizabeth?

ELIZABETH. Yes, sir?

JACK. With a new staff member in the household – I'm sure you understand the importance of discretion.

ELIZABETH. Oh, yes sir. Do you mean...?

JACK. Yes. You and I have spoken somewhat freely about my concern for my wife's state of mind. You wouldn't...

ELIZABETH. Oh, no. I would never repeat that.

JACK. Thank you. I knew I could rely on you.

(**ELIZABETH** *starts to leave, but* **JACK** *stops her.*)

And of course, that includes not only what's happened – what you've seen – but also what I've told you about her mother.

ELIZABETH. Oh yes. The poor woman. I would never talk about that, sir. Imagine your own mother being put away like that.

JACK. I know. And now, Bella – I can't help wondering if...

ELIZABETH. Oh.

JACK. I know. I wish I'd never even thought it.

ELIZABETH. I'll do everything I can to protect your privacy, sir – yours and Mrs. Manningham's.

JACK. Thank you, Elizabeth. Your kindness makes all the difference.

(**ELIZABETH** *exits.* **JACK** *is left alone in the drawing room.*)

(*After a few moments,* **BELLA** *enters.*)

BELLA. How was your morning?

JACK. It was good. Busy. And how are you feeling?

BELLA. Fine, I'm fine. It's a beautiful day. Why don't we take a walk in the park?

JACK. Oh! Yes, of course, if you –

BELLA. I do. I feel fine. I just need a few minutes to get ready.

(She busies herself to cover her distress.)

JACK. Have you got the mail?

BELLA. Oh, no. I didn't think of it yet. Are you expecting something?

JACK. Nothing special. Ring for Nancy to bring it up.

BELLA. Oh, that's all right. I can get it from Elizabeth.

JACK. Bella, this is precisely why we hired that girl. To take these little errands off your hands. Ring the bell.

BELLA. I can do it.

JACK. Bella: you are the mistress of this house. Show the staff that you are in charge.

*(Beat. **BELLA** rings the bell.)*

Well done.

*(**NANCY** enters.)*

NANCY. Yes?

BELLA. Nancy, would you please bring up this morning's mail?

NANCY. Of course, ma'am.

(She goes.)

*(**JACK** crosses to her.)*

JACK. That was very mistressy. Madam.

BELLA. *(Laughs uncertainly.)* I don't know why I –

> *(**NANCY** returns.)*

NANCY. Here you are.

> *(She brings the mail to **JACK**, passing **BELLA** by.)*

JACK. Thank you Nancy. Very much appreciated.

NANCY. Not at all, sir. My pleasure.

JACK. Settling in all right, are you?

NANCY. Yes, sir. It's a lovely house. I've never had such a nice bedroom.

> *(She curtsies flirtatiously to **JACK**, then briefly to **BELLA** before exiting.)*

BELLA. Jack.

JACK. Mm?

BELLA. May I see the mail?

JACK. Of course!

BELLA. Jack, how can you – did you see that look she gave me? Don't you see how she – how she *behaves*?

JACK. What do you mean?

BELLA. She takes liberties. The way she looks at you.

JACK. Bella. I am very flattered that you think I could be an object of interest to a young girl, but...*don't*.

BELLA. But I'm not –

JACK. For one thing, anyone can see that all my thoughts are with you. *Please* don't –

BELLA. Of course not, I was just – It was silly, I –

(She notices a letter among the others; in amazement:)

Look at this, Jack. It's an invitation!

JACK. What?

BELLA. An invitation! To a party!

JACK. Why would –

BELLA. A birthday party for a friend of my father's. Lady Margaret Beech. How did she find me, after all this time?

JACK. Margaret Beech. Who –?

BELLA. I knew her here in London when I was a girl. In fact, she's my godmother, though we lost touch, I don't know why.

JACK. Good heavens, you're full of surprises, aren't you.

BELLA. Jack, we must go!

JACK. Bella...

BELLA. It would mean so much to me. We haven't had any invitations, no one visits here, and I know why that is, I do, but it would be so wonderful to see an old friend.

JACK. But don't you think –

BELLA. Please. Just for a little while.

JACK. Well, if you think you can manage it...

BELLA. I can. I can. I want to be out where there are other people again!

JACK. All right.

(He takes the invitation from her.)

I'll tell her we are coming.

BELLA. Oh, thank you! Thank you!

JACK. Not wearing your lovely pearls today, my dear?

BELLA. What? Oh. I must not have put them on this morning. You won't be sorry, Jack. This makes me so happy.

(**BELLA** *exits.* **JACK** *watches her go.*)

Scene Three

(The next evening.)

*(**BELLA** rummages through the sofa cushions, stops guiltily as **JACK** enters.)*

JACK. There you are. Didn't you hear me calling you?

BELLA. I – no, I'm sorry, I didn't.

JACK. Is something wrong? What are you doing?

BELLA. Oh, Jack! The pearls. My mother's pearls. I – I can't find them. I've looked everywhere.

JACK. Oh dear. Let's just think this through. You've hardly left the house recently, so they must be here somewhere.

BELLA. Yes, yes – that's right, they must be.

JACK. And you haven't taken them off during the day to look at them, or –

BELLA. No. I'm sure I haven't. They are precious to me, I would never... I took them off to sleep, and to bathe. But that's all.

JACK. And when did you last see them?

BELLA. I'm not sure. This morning they weren't on my bureau, and then I couldn't remember taking them off last night, so I thought the catch might have broken and they were here somewhere...but they're not.

JACK. *(Lifting a cushion.)* You're sure?

BELLA. Yes. Yes. They're not here, I've been looking for them all day. I've asked Elizabeth, and Nancy, and – and... Jack, do you think it's possible that Nancy could have...

JACK. Could have what?

BELLA. Well – could have taken them. I'm not saying she has, but I've looked everywhere, and there must be some explanation...

JACK. Bella. I know you don't much care for Nancy. But to accuse the staff of theft, especially when you yourself have been –

BELLA. I know. I know. It's just I *know* I didn't leave them somewhere, and I can't believe I would have *hidden* them, not those pearls, surely not. And Nancy hasn't been with us long, we really don't know her, it's the only explanation I can –

JACK. Call her in.

BELLA. What do you mean?

JACK. If you think the staff may be stealing from us, we must find out. Call them both in.

BELLA. But I don't want –

JACK. I know you don't. But this is serious. How can we have a staff that we cannot trust?

BELLA. It's – it's not –

JACK. Bella. If you think Nancy, or Elizabeth for that matter, could have taken your pearls, we must get to the bottom of it immediately. Remember, you are the mistress of this house.

> (**BELLA** *moves to the call bell and pulls it. They wait in silence. After a moment,* **ELIZABETH** *enters.*)

Elizabeth, will you and Nancy please come here to the sitting room?

ELIZABETH. Yes, sir.

> (**ELIZABETH** *exits. Again,* **BELLA** *and* **JACK** *wait in silence.*)

*(**ELIZABETH** and **NANCY** enter.)*

Yes, sir? You wanted to see us.

JACK. Actually, it is Mrs. Manningham. Isn't that right, Bella?

Go ahead, dear.

BELLA. My – my pearls...

JACK. Speak up, please. Elizabeth and Nancy can't answer if they can't hear you.

BELLA. My pearls... I was – I was looking for...

ELIZABETH. Yes, ma'am? Your pearl necklace that was misplaced. Have you found it yet?

BELLA. No, I...

JACK. Mrs. Manningham wishes to know whether one of you may have taken her necklace.

*(**ELIZABETH** gasps.)*

BELLA. I just – I wondered –

ELIZABETH. No sir, Mr. Manningham, I did not touch any of Mrs. Manningham's jewelry.

NANCY. Nor did I.

ELIZABETH. Will that be all, sir?

JACK. *(Looking at **BELLA**.)* Not quite. I believe Mrs. Manningham needs some more assurance. Elizabeth, will you please fetch the Bible off the bookshelf there?

*(**ELIZABETH** does so.)*

Now will you place your hand on it, please, and give us your oath that you did not take Mrs. Manningham's pearl necklace.

*(**ELIZABETH** places her hand on the Bible.)*

ELIZABETH. *(Neutral.)* I swear that I did not take Mrs. Manningham's pearl necklace.

JACK. Thank you. And you as well, please, Nancy.

NANCY. Yes, sir. *(She places her hand on the Bible.)* I swear that I did not take Mrs. Manningham's pearl necklace. *(Beat.)* If *I'd* done it I'd've –

JACK. That is all, Nancy. You may go.

> (**ELIZABETH** *and* **NANCY** *go out,* **ELIZABETH** *closing the doors.* **JACK** *picks up the Bible.*)

I hope that will ease your mind.

BELLA. *(Crossing to* **JACK**.*)* Give me that!

> *(She snatches the Bible from him and places her hand on it.)*

I swear that I did not hide my pearl necklace. I didn't. I did not, I know that's what you're thinking but –

JACK. Bella...

BELLA. I swear to God that I don't know where it is. *(Holding the Bible.)* I swear it! What else do you want me to do? I'll swear on my –

JACK. For God's sake!

BELLA. Jack, I will –

JACK. *Stop it!* Of course you did it. You've hidden the pearls, the same as you moved that picture and hid the grocery bill –

BELLA. Jack please! I –

JACK. *(His voice rising.)* – *and* my pocket watch, and all those other things, again and again – it never ends. And now you blame the staff for your own –

BELLA. *(Clutching at him.)* Please! I didn't – I'm not –

JACK. Stop it! *(Grabs her by the arms.)* Enough! Look at you! Stop lying to yourself. You're irrational. You've lost your senses. Like your mother.

> *(**BELLA** slumps.)*

I'm sorry. I'm sorry. That was – I shouldn't have said that. But I'm afraid... I'm afraid that one day I will not be able to protect you anymore.

BELLA. *(Softly.)* Please help me. I don't know what to do.

JACK. I know. And I know you're trying. I shouldn't have lost my temper. It's hard... I find it hard. But I have to do better.

> *(He helps her to a seat.)*

Now. It's getting to be dark out. Nancy will be here in a moment to light the gas. I'm sorry to have to do this, but I must go out for a while.

BELLA. No...

JACK. I must.

BELLA. Please don't leave me here. Jack, please.

JACK. I have an appointment with a buyer at the club, Bella. It is terrible timing, but you know I cannot miss it.

> *(**NANCY** enters and lights the gas, sneaking a curious look at **JACK** and **BELLA**. They wait somewhat awkwardly until she exits.)*

All right. Why don't you lie down right here on the sofa.

> *(**BELLA** moves to the sofa.)*

BELLA. Don't go! I hate when you leave me alone here. It's frightening, I –

JACK. There is nothing to be frightened of.

BELLA. I don't feel safe. I can't be by myself. I need – Jack, where is your gun? Is it still in the desk? Give it to me – in case...

JACK. My gun? Bella. I can't just hand that over, especially to someone who – who hasn't been trained to use it.

BELLA. But I have been. Remember? My father taught me. Please let me have it, I'll just keep it nearby in case – in case –

JACK. In case what?

BELLA. I don't know. In case I need it. If you're going to leave me here alone –

JACK. But you're not alone, you have Elizabeth and Nancy.

BELLA. It's Nancy's night out. She'll be going now.

JACK. Elizabeth then. If you need anything, you can ring for her. What is this really about? Is something frightening you when you're alone?

BELLA. I – never mind. I just – it must be – it's all in my head. But if you could come home tonight as soon as you can, as soon as your meetings are finished – I would be so grateful.

JACK. Of course. You know I wouldn't go at all if it weren't absolutely necessary.

BELLA. Thank you. *(She takes his hand.)* I don't know what I'd do without you.

JACK. Sit tight. I'll be home as soon as I can.

> (**JACK** *exits.*)

> (**BELLA** *stands for a moment, looking after him. She paces the room, trying to calm herself. She might look out the window, pull the curtains, check that the door is locked, or look in the mirror and try to pull herself together. Maybe she sits down and tries*

*to read a book. But the stress is too much:
eventually she jumps up, crosses to Jack's
desk and tries to open the drawer where she
thinks his gun is kept, but it is locked.)*

*(A thump is heard from above, and then
another. **BELLA** freezes.)*

*(It is hard to tell if these sounds are real, or
imaginary.)*

BELLA. *(Very tense.)* Hello? Is someone –

*(Another muffled thud, and what might be
footsteps. The gaslight dims perceptibly.
BELLA closes her eyes.)*

Oh no…

*(More thumps and thuds, or perhaps the
sound of something being dragged, slowly.)*

Not tonight… I can't…

*(The sounds continue. **BELLA** paces the room,
tries to block them out. Finally, she runs to
the call bell and pulls it.)*

*(**ELIZABETH** enters.)*

ELIZABETH. You rang, Mrs. Manningham?

BELLA. Yes, Elizabeth. Thank you. Elizabeth, I'm – I'm
sorry, about…

ELIZABETH. That's all right, ma'am. I've nothing to hide,
so I don't mind being asked.

*(Beat. It's impossible to tell whether **ELIZABETH**
is offended.)*

BELLA. Elizabeth, I am sorry to bother you but I – can you –
can you hear something?

ELIZABETH. Ma'am?

BELLA. Yes, a thumping or thudding from above. It echoes down here from the attic, can't you hear? Footsteps, or... As if there's someone moving around, or something being dragged.

ELIZABETH. I'm sorry, ma'am. I don't hear anything. But then, my hearing's not what it should be.

BELLA. It isn't? Why?

ELIZABETH. I was ill as a child, you know, and it went into my ears so to speak.

BELLA. I'm sorry, I didn't know. Why didn't I know that?

ELIZABETH. Oh, it's all right. I get by just fine, here in the house. I hear when people speak to me, 'specially if I can see their faces, and I can hear the bell of course, it's quite loud below stairs.

BELLA. It's strange that I didn't know this before.

ELIZABETH. Not at all, ma'am. I'm able to do my job, so why would you?

BELLA. I suppose.

ELIZABETH. Miss Alice, Alice Barlow, who owned this house – she in the portrait, she were awful kind to me about it.

BELLA. *(Turning to the portrait.)* Was she?

ELIZABETH. Oh, yes. She took me in to work here when I was just a girl, and she helped me learn how to listen for the things I needed to hear.

BELLA. She has a nice face, so lively and...

ELIZABETH. Kind. That's it, ma'am. She were lively, and kind.

BELLA. I'm so sorry – what happened to Miss Alice. What a terrible thing.

ELIZABETH. Yes, it was. And of course, I was responsible.

BELLA. You? But how?

ELIZABETH. Well, I didn't hear anything, did I? Right upstairs I was, in my room, when it happened.

BELLA. And you didn't...

ELIZABETH. I didn't hear a thing, Mrs. Not a thing. And I can't help but think, if Miss Alice weren't so kind, finding a place in her home for a housekeeper that can't hear everything just right –

BELLA. Oh, but you mustn't –

ELIZABETH. – then maybe she'd still be alive today.

BELLA. Oh, Elizabeth.

ELIZABETH. She'd have had another housekeeper, and that housekeeper would've heard her call for help, and gone for the police, and...

BELLA. *(Taking* **ELIZABETH***'s hand.)* Elizabeth. What happened was terrible. But you mustn't blame yourself. Who's to say what another housekeeper might have done?

> *(They sit for a moment. Then* **ELIZABETH** *wipes her eyes.)*

ELIZABETH. Yes of course, you're right. There's just no telling how things will turn out, one moment to the next, is there Mrs.?

BELLA. No, there isn't.

ELIZABETH. And...things aren't always quite as they seem to be, are they.

BELLA. Why, no, surely not.

ELIZABETH. No.

BELLA. What things, Elizabeth? What do you mean?

ELIZABETH. Oh, nothing in particular, ma'am. Just...we must always be paying attention, and asking ourselves questions about what we see and hear, isn't that right ma'am?

BELLA. Well, I suppose...

ELIZABETH. And trusting our own thoughts about what is what.

BELLA. *(A bit puzzled.)* Yes.

(Brief pause.)

Elizabeth?

ELIZABETH. Yes, ma'am?

BELLA. I know you don't hear these strange sounds, and perhaps it really is my imagination. But do you see, look, the gaslight. It goes down.

ELIZABETH. It goes –?

BELLA. Down. Yes. At night, when I am alone. Just a little bit. Can you see it? Right now, it's down.

ELIZABETH. I'm sorry ma'am, I can't say that I do see. If it's just a little bit, then perhaps I've never noticed.

BELLA. You can't see that the light is lower in here than it was before? As if someone, somewhere in the house, had turned on another light?

ELIZABETH. Someone in another room?

BELLA. You know how that happens, when someone turns a light on, the lights in every room dip just a bit.

ELIZABETH. Oh yes. Because the pressure goes down on the gas. Miss Alice explained that to me when she had it installed. Well, it might be a little darker, ma'am. But I couldn't say for certain.

BELLA. It sounds as if there's someone here.

ELIZABETH. Someone here in the house, Mrs.?

BELLA. Above. Someone – or something – that waits for Jack to go out, waits until I am alone, and then begins shuffling and dragging about, and makes it go darker in here, and –

ELIZABETH. But Mrs., it –

BELLA. I know it sounds mad, but – I think there is something, someone, up in the attic. Could that be possible?

ELIZABETH. I don't know, ma'am. I don't see how that could be. The door to the attic is sealed up. We pass it every day. You know the one.

BELLA. Yes.

ELIZABETH. After she died, Miss Alice's things were moved up there and the attic was sealed off. I just kept this portrait down here, to remember her, and a few other things.

BELLA. I see.

ELIZABETH. *(Carefully.)* I hope you don't mind its being here.

BELLA. I don't. I know it must seem... well, since I keep removing it, and hiding it... though I don't... *(Looks at the picture.)* I don't mind the portrait. It's beautiful. And look at the jewels she's wearing.

ELIZABETH. I sometimes wish they weren't in the picture.

BELLA. Why?

ELIZABETH. Because that's why she died. Those rubies. Didn't you know, ma'am? That's what he – the killer – was after, when he broke in.

BELLA. Oh. I see.

ELIZABETH. He tore up this room, and broke open the safe, and took the rubies and some bank notes that were in there. That's what the police said.

BELLA. How dreadful. One almost wishes she had never had the rubies to begin with.

ELIZABETH. Yes. One does. But don't you worry, ma'am. That attic's well locked up. I just don't see how anyone could get in there without our knowing.

BELLA. Of course. Then it's only my imagination, those noises... they've stopped now, do you hear?

(*They listen again. Nothing.*)

Some nights I just sit here and listen. It...it fills me with such dread, Elizabeth, I cannot tell you.

ELIZABETH. Do you suppose, ma'am...

BELLA. What?

ELIZABETH. I only wondered, ma'am, whether it's – being here. In this house.

BELLA. Oh. Do you mean it's...

ELIZABETH. I don't know how I do it myself, sometimes, stay here I mean, knowing what happened.

BELLA. And why do you?

ELIZABETH. I suppose I felt someone had to look after Miss Alice's home for her, even if she's gone, and it's let out by an estate company now.

BELLA. That's very...

ELIZABETH. But I only wonder sometimes, ma'am, if a house like this is the best place for you. It's rather dark and gloomy, isn't it, and then the murder...

BELLA. Yes. You're right. We – Jack, it was Jack – he wanted so badly to live here.

ELIZABETH. Yes?

BELLA. He told me he had found us a house in London, and it was affordable, and such a beautiful neighbourhood... but we could have...

ELIZABETH. Ma'am?

BELLA. I don't think Mr. Manningham had a nice home to live in, when he was a boy.

(Suddenly.) I haven't been a helpful wife and partner to him, Elizabeth, not the way I wanted to be or the way I think he would wish.

ELIZABETH. Now, Mrs...

BELLA. I don't have a large inheritance, or a title or... I can't bear to take this away from him, this house. You see how much he loves it here.

ELIZABETH. And what does Mr. Manningham say about the noises?

BELLA. If only it would happen while he's here, but it never does. Never. No one hears it except me. I haven't told him. I haven't told anyone, except you, now. I'm afraid that if Jack knew I was hearing things, he would give up on me altogether.

ELIZABETH. Oh ma'am. Don't cry. There, there. You'll be all right.

BELLA. Yes. Thank you.

I should get some rest. Jack said... Elizabeth –

ELIZABETH. Don't you worry, ma'am. I won't say a word. You have a good sleep now.

> (**ELIZABETH** *is exiting.* **BELLA** *notices the gaslight going up again.)*

BELLA. Elizabeth! Elizabeth, did you –

> (**ELIZABETH** *has gone.)*

Scene Four

(A few days later. Early evening. The room is empty.)

*(**BELLA** calls from the foyer.)*

BELLA. Jack? Jack? I'm sorry I'm late, I couldn't find a cab anywhere.

(She enters the drawing room, carrying packages.)

*(**BELLA** takes a small box out of her packages, admires it, and places it on the mantel. **JACK** enters in evening wear.)*

JACK. There you are. You're not dressed! We don't want to be late.

BELLA. No, no. I promise I'll be ready soon. I just felt so happy today, I wanted it to last.

JACK. I'm so glad to hear that, my dear.

BELLA. I want to tell you something.

JACK. What is it?

BELLA. Jack. I know these last few months have been difficult.

JACK. Oh Bella...

BELLA. They have, Jack. I sometimes feel as though you and I are speaking different languages. Like we don't understand the heart of what each of us is trying to say. But we can still – Do you remember the day we met?

JACK. Of course I do. By the lake.

BELLA. And how happy we were?

(He smiles at her.)

JACK. You were the most beautiful...

BELLA. But since we came here, with all that has happened – to me – with me – how I've changed...it has seemed as though that happiness is gone forever...

JACK. Darling, it's not your fault.

BELLA. As though after all of our – *my* – troubles, we can never see each other in that same golden light again.

JACK. Bella...

BELLA. But I'm not giving up. We are still the same people who fell in love with each other. And I love you as much as I ever did.

JACK. You are my angel, Bella. And if I have ever –

BELLA. But two people that love each other must choose love.

JACK. And I do. I choose you. I have chosen you every day.

BELLA. Yes! We must choose it again, and again. I see that. Today, thinking about going with you to this party, sitting with you, and whispering our little secrets, like we did before we were married, introducing you to people from my life before I knew you, and knitting that life and this life together...it made me so happy. I choose it. I choose you. We can put the past few months behind us and start fresh.

JACK. Of course.

BELLA. Look!

(She gets the box from the mantel.)

I have something for you.

(He opens it.)

JACK. Cuff links.

BELLA. *(Quickly.)* I know you have cuff links already. But these are new ones. For a new start. Choosing a new start. Do you see?

JACK. Yes, I see.

BELLA. I know we can do it. I can do it.

JACK. *(Looking into her eyes.)* Nothing could make me happier.

BELLA. Thank you, Jack. I love you.

> *(They kiss. **BELLA** jumps up.)*

I won't be long!

> *(**BELLA** exits.)*

> *(**JACK** pours himself a drink, takes the cuff links out of the box, and examines them. He swaps them for his own, at some point taking a moment to call up the stairs.)*

JACK. Bella, come along my darling! We don't want to keep the driver waiting!

> *(There is no response.)*

> *(As he finishes changing his cuff links, **NANCY** enters and lights the gas. **JACK** glances at her.)*

NANCY. I suppose you'll be leaving soon, then, Mr. Manningham, sir.

JACK. Yes. Just as soon as she's ready.

NANCY. It sounds like it'll be a nice party.

JACK. I certainly hope so.

NANCY. Mrs. Manningham seems to be looking forward to it. She has a new dress, and all.

(No comment from **JACK**. **NANCY** *finishes her task and turns to face him.)*

Is there anything else you want. Sir.

*(***JACK*** *hands her his empty glass. He might be about to speak, when* **BELLA** *returns in her party attire.* **JACK** *goes to her, takes her hand, and kisses it.)*

JACK. You are...beautiful.

BELLA. I'm so happy. I hear that is the best addition to any ensemble.

(She notices **NANCY** *is still there.)*

Thank you, Nancy. That will be all for tonight.

*(***NANCY*** *goes out,* **BELLA** *too flushed with excitement to notice her any further.)*

JACK. You're sure you are up to this.

BELLA. I am. *(Noticing the cuff links.)* We are.

JACK. Yes.

*(***BELLA*** *gets her evening bag, and* **JACK** *puts a lace shawl around her shoulders.)*

BELLA. I can't wait to introduce you to Lady Margaret. She will adore you. She's such a good judge of character.

JACK. Come along, chatterbox. The party will be over before we get there!

(They exit together.)

Scene Five

(Hours later, around ten o'clock at night. Outside, darkness and rain, with the occasional rumble of thunder.)

(We hear **BELLA** and **JACK** before we see them.)

BELLA. Jack – please Jack, no – wait –

JACK. For God's sake, Bella, come inside.

(They enter. Both are damp from the rain. **BELLA** has been crying and is disheveled. She puts her handbag down somewhere in the room.)

BELLA. If you'd just listen, Jack.

JACK. There's really nothing to be said.

BELLA. But I –

JACK. I know you've been trying. So have I. I've done everything I can – I've tried to protect you, to be understanding and patient. But I don't know what more I can do.

BELLA. You only [need to] –

JACK. On a night like this – to be up to those same tricks and irrational – It's too much. You must see that.

BELLA. Yes. I do. Please...

JACK. You'd better go to bed. We'll talk in the morning.

(Thunder.)

BELLA. Yes.

(**BELLA** slowly climbs the stairs. **ELIZABETH** enters. **BELLA** pauses and overhears the following.)

ELIZABETH. Back so early, sir? Is anything wrong?

JACK. I'm afraid it is. *(He sighs deeply.)* It was very unfortunate.

ELIZABETH. Oh, dear.

JACK. While dinner was being served, one of the guests noticed that her gold bracelet was missing. She was very upset. Servants were asked to assist, and a scene played out in our hostess's dining room that was not unlike the one you were subjected to not long ago, here in this room.

ELIZABETH. Oh.

JACK. Except this time, after the servants had been all but accused of theft, the bracelet was discovered – by accident – in Mrs. Manningham's evening bag.

ELIZABETH. Oh my – oh dear.

JACK. Indeed.

I don't need to tell you how deeply embarrassing this was for all concerned. Lady Margaret's image of her goddaughter must be irrevocably altered.

What a terrible disappointment this evening has been – for all of us.

(Thunder.)

ELIZABETH. It all seems very sad, sir.

JACK. I'm at my wits' end, Elizabeth.

ELIZABETH. Yes, sir.

JACK. I – we – have tried everything, haven't we? Kindness, patience – even firmness. At some point, we will need to get help.

ELIZABETH. Sir?

JACK. It's difficult to speak of this. But you and I both know that there are places where Mrs. Manningham can be prevented from harming herself, and others.

ELIZABETH. I... yes, sir.

(**BELLA**, *apparently unseen, is still listening.*)

JACK. I'm sorry for what happened the other day.

ELIZABETH. It's all –

JACK. No. It isn't all right. Bella should never have accused you, or Nancy, when we all know – don't we – that her mother's pearls were taken and put somewhere, by Mrs. Manningham herself.

ELIZABETH. Oh, dear. I hope not, sir.

JACK. Just as that gold bracelet was. Heaven knows why. I wish I knew why.

ELIZABETH. Yes, sir.

JACK. We won't give up yet. But we must be ready, when the time comes. Mustn't we, Elizabeth?

ELIZABETH. Yes, sir. We will be.

JACK. Good.

Well – I am going out. Despite the weather! I'm going to try to forget, for a little while. I'll be at my club. Do you think it's wrong? To go out tonight, when my wife is so...

ELIZABETH. Oh, no, sir. No.

JACK. Thank you. You're very kind. Well, good night.

ELIZABETH. Good night, sir.

(**JACK** *exits.* **ELIZABETH** *stands looking for a moment at the portrait of Alice Barlow, then exits.*)

(**BELLA** *descends the stairs and comes into the room, trembling. She picks up her evening bag and stares at it uncomprehendingly – she cannot remember taking the bracelet.*)

(*She paces the room. The storm outside grows, we hear thunder and see flashes of lightning.* **BELLA** *jumps, frightened. She tries to calm herself. She stands still, trying desperately to remember.*)

(*Suddenly, the gaslight goes down. Creaks and groans come from overhead, as if something heavy is being moved, or perhaps it is the creaking and groaning of the house itself, magnified in her mind.* **BELLA** *covers her ears, as the wind howls outside, and we hear what might be chattering whispers or perhaps tree branches brushing against the house.*)

BELLA. No... Please stop, please!

(*Thunder crashes.* **BELLA** *looks desperately about the room. Her gaze falls on Jack's desk. She rushes to it and struggles to open a drawer. It is locked. She finds the letter opener and uses it to pick the lock.*)

(*With the drawer open,* **BELLA** *pulls out Jack's revolver. The noises from above are reaching a crescendo. She holds the gun out to protect herself from the unseen enemy.*)

(*A terrible idea occurs to her. Sobbing, she raises the gun to her temple. The thunder startles her and she pulls the gun away from her head, frightened now by what she has almost done.*)

(**BELLA** *takes a shaky breath, turns to put the gun back – and finds something else in the open drawer. She freezes.*)

(**BELLA** *slowly pulls her mother's pearls from Jack's drawer. She holds the pearls up, staring at them. Lightning and a final crash of thunder.*)

End Act One

ACT TWO

Scene One

*(The next morning. **JACK** alone at the table with a cup of tea and the paper. Nothing in the room has changed: Jack's desk is exactly as it was before **BELLA** opened the drawer. **ELIZABETH** enters.)*

ELIZABETH. Has Mrs. Manningham not been down yet, sir?

JACK. She has not.

ELIZABETH. Should I look in on her, do you think?

BELLA. *(On the stairs.)* No need.

> *(**BELLA** enters. She is doing her best to seem composed.)*

JACK. There you are, dear. I was beginning to worry. You've missed breakfast!

ELIZABETH. Can I get you something, ma'am?

BELLA. I don't feel hungry just now, but tea would be lovely, thank you Elizabeth.

ELIZABETH. Of course.

> *(**ELIZABETH** exits.)*

JACK. Did you sleep well? You look a bit pale.

BELLA. I suppose I didn't sleep very much. But I'm feeling all right.

(**BELLA** *sits at the table.* **ELIZABETH** *brings her a cup of tea.*)

ELIZABETH. Will that be all for now, ma'am?

BELLA. Yes. I'll speak to you later in the morning about dinner.

ELIZABETH. Yes, ma'am.

JACK. Won't you have something to eat, Bella?

BELLA. No thank you.

(**ELIZABETH** *exits.*)

JACK. About last night...

BELLA. It's all right, Jack.

JACK. All right?

BELLA. I apologize for my – for the incident at the party. I thought I was ready to join the world again. But now I see that you were right.

JACK. What do you mean?

BELLA. I need more rest, more...time.

JACK. More time, yes. That's right, dear.

BELLA. You know Jack, it's strange.

JACK. What is?

BELLA. I feel as if, each time I begin to get better – to feel more like myself – that's when something happens.

JACK. What happens?

BELLA. Something happens, and it all falls apart.

JACK. Something happens? Or you *do* something? Are you saying that...

BELLA. That it wasn't I who moved the picture from the wall, or took that bracelet, or hid my mother's pearls... we don't know where... No, I'm not saying that. Who could it be, if not me?

(She is watching him carefully, but not obviously.)

JACK. I don't know. We've already asked the staff, but they could be lying, I suppose. Do you want to ask them again?

BELLA. No. Not at all.

JACK. We could search their rooms, if you...

BELLA. That won't be necessary. Please don't.

JACK. Well, all right. If you're satisfied. But doesn't that leave us back where we started? If it's not the staff, and not you – or me, of course –

BELLA. You? Well, that's silly. Why would you do such a thing?

JACK. Indeed.

BELLA. But really. Why *would* you?

JACK. Why would I what?

BELLA. Why would you take my things, or your own for that matter, and hide them away, and pretend it was someone else?

JACK. Well, precisely. What reason could I possibly have?

BELLA. Precisely. Then again, what reason could I have?

JACK. None at all, Bella. Just as your poor mother had no reason for any of *her* behaviour. What is this –

BELLA. I wish I had never told you about my mother.

JACK. Oh, don't wish that. If I didn't know about it, think of all the time we would have wasted! The staff would all have been dismissed, and I would be checking the window latches for break-ins. This way, we know where to start. Instead of blaming others, we can concentrate on helping *you*.

BELLA. Yes. It's important to know where to start, isn't it?

JACK. Certainly.

BELLA. And then – and then what?

JACK. I don't...?

BELLA. Once you know who is doing it, that it's me I mean – then what do you do?

JACK. Well, as you know, we have hoped that with the love and support of myself and the staff, you will be able to recover yourself. That is still the hope, of course. But if this continues – the emotions, the strange pranks –

BELLA. My pearls –

JACK. Yes, your pearls of all things, I know how much you treasure them – even *they* are fodder for these delusions and tricks.

BELLA. And you don't know where they are?

JACK. What? The pearls?

BELLA. *(Clinging to hope.)* Yes. You didn't put them away somewhere, to teach me a lesson, or to keep them safe, or –

JACK. Of course not. You've hidden them away, I'm afraid, and you don't remember it, as always. We can only hope they'll come to light soon.

BELLA. But...

JACK. Are you sure you are all right this morning?

BELLA. No.

JACK. You seem very emotional. Why don't you go back upstairs. Rest some more.

BELLA. Yes. I'm fine. I'll just go and... Excuse me.

*(**BELLA** runs out. **JACK** looks after her.)*

Scene Two

*(That evening. **NANCY** lights the gas. **JACK** enters and **NANCY** curtsies to him self-consciously. He watches her exit, then turns to stare at the portrait of Alice Barlow. **BELLA** enters. **JACK** crosses to busy himself at his desk.)*

JACK. Feeling better, dear?

BELLA. *(A bit distracted.)* Yes. Thank you... Are you going out this evening?

JACK. I'm afraid I must. I'm sorry that I won't be able to spend the evening with you.

BELLA. Mm. *(Realizing that **JACK** is expecting a different response.)* Oh – don't go, Jack! Please stay in tonight. You know how I hate to be left alone here.

JACK. I'll come home as soon as I can, my dear. I always do.

BELLA. Yes. Of course. I just... I don't know what I'd do without you. But where are you going?

JACK. To meet a friend of mine, at the club.

BELLA. The club. That's where you always go, when you go out, isn't it?

JACK. Of course it is. You know that.

BELLA. And what do you do, there?

JACK. Bella, you know what I do. I take care of our business. Tonight I'll be getting some advice on...a complicated matter, it's nothing you need to worry about.

BELLA. No, of course. You know best, dear. Good night.

JACK. Good night, Bella.

*(**JACK** exits. We hear the front door close.)*

(**BELLA** *hurries to the window and looks through the curtains, quietly opens the door and checks the hallway. Satisfied that no one is near, she approaches Jack's desk. She pulls out the letter opener and again picks the lock, gently sliding the drawer open. She finds the pearl necklace still there. She looks through the drawer, but there is nothing else of interest. After a moment's thought, she returns the necklace to its place and relocks the drawer.*)

(*She looks overhead and waits. There are no sounds. This is not what she expected. She stands very still, listening, for the first time hoping, to hear those sounds. She watches the gaslight for a moment, then closes her eyes to listen again. Nothing.*)

(**NANCY** *enters, jumping when she sees* **BELLA**.)

NANCY. Oh! Ma'am, I didn't realize –

BELLA. Yes, Nancy? Is there something you need?

(**BELLA** *notices that* **NANCY** *is holding a sherry glass. It is clear that she has been helping herself.*)

Have you come to return that glass?

NANCY. Oh, yes. I just – I meant to put it –

BELLA. On the sideboard will be fine.

(**NANCY** *crosses to the sideboard.*)

Where did you get the glass, Nancy? Or when, I should say? If you don't mind my asking.

NANCY. It was Mr. Manningham, ma'am.

BELLA. I see.

NANCY. Yes. He told me to. The master said I should try a taste of sherry if I hadn't already, and he gave me a glass. Earlier this evening, ma'am.

BELLA. I'll take it up with my husband, then. When he gets home.

NANCY. Yes, ma'am.

>   (**ELIZABETH** *enters.*)

ELIZABETH. *(To **NANCY**.)* There you are! What are you doing in here, bothering the Mrs.?

NANCY. Just tidying.

ELIZABETH. Well, since you're of a mind to tidy, you can go to the kitchen and empty the scrap-bucket. Into the bin in the lane.

>   (**NANCY** *almost rebels, but…*)

NANCY. Yes, missus.

ELIZABETH. And when you're done with that, you can clear out the kitchen stove. Mind you save those ashes.

>   (**NANCY** *seethes her way out of the room.*)

I'm sorry, ma'am. I don't have Nancy trained properly yet. You leave it with me, she'll soon be toeing the line.

BELLA. Thank you, Elizabeth. Perhaps I'll speak to Mr. Manningham as well.

ELIZABETH. If that girl were a year or two younger, I'd take her over my knee.

BELLA. I admit I would like to see that!

ELIZABETH. Is there anything I can get for you, ma'am?

BELLA. Oh no, thank you, I'm fine.

ELIZABETH. Not hearing any…anything untoward, from upstairs, this evening, are you?

BELLA. No, I haven't. It's strange. I thought I would hear it tonight.

> *(They both pause for a moment,* **BELLA** *listening,* **ELIZABETH** *waiting.)*

Nothing.

Do you know, Elizabeth, I had almost persuaded myself that it was real. That there was someone – up there.

ELIZABETH. Oh dear. I hope not, ma'am!

BELLA. I even thought I might know who it was. Or could be. But for the life of me I couldn't see why. And now I wonder if I did imagine it, after all.

Does it frighten you? The idea that someone could be up in the attic?

ELIZABETH. I can't hardly think of it without a shiver going up the spine.

BELLA. But do you know what is more frightening than that? More frightening than the thought that there might be someone moving about in our house at night?

ELIZABETH. What?

BELLA. *That there isn't.*

ELIZABETH. Ma'am?

BELLA. That there's nobody there at all...except in my mind. That, Elizabeth...*that* is frightening.

ELIZABETH. I was wondering, ma'am, if you'd given any thought to being here. Only I wonder if a change of scenery –

BELLA. Yes. I have thought... *(Listens again.)* There really isn't any noise above us, is there?

ELIZABETH. Well, not that I can hear, but –

BELLA. But Mr. Manningham, he's gone out, he did go out, did he not?

ELIZABETH. Oh yes.

BELLA. Elizabeth, may I ask you something?

ELIZABETH. Of course, ma'am.

BELLA. My mother – I think my husband must have told you that she wasn't always well. He has spoken of it, hasn't he?

ELIZABETH. He did mention. It's very sad, ma'am.

BELLA. Yes. I missed her dreadfully, when she was taken away. I felt so alone. Of course I was only small at the time.

ELIZABETH. That's when we need them most.

BELLA. Mr. Manningham, I know he worries –

ELIZABETH. Yes?

BELLA. My mother was nervous, they said. She didn't like to be with people. She was fearful, and it grew and grew, until she couldn't – even for me, she couldn't...

And I am like her, Elizabeth, do you see? I can't bear to be with people. I'm nervous, all the time. I am fearful.

ELIZABETH. No, ma'am. You are not like her.

Scene Three

(The next morning. The room is empty.)

*(**BELLA** enters, looking tired. She paces the room. Stares at Jack's desk. She jumps a little as **JACK** enters.)*

JACK. Good morning. You're up early.

BELLA. Yes. How was your evening? At your – at the club?

JACK. Much the same as always.

*(**BELLA** pours herself some tea.)*

Why don't you and I go for a walk this afternoon.

BELLA. I don't think so. Thank you, though.

JACK. Very well.

(He sits at his desk and looks at her.)

You are looking very thoughtful, my dear. What is on your mind?

BELLA. Nothing... Do you remember when you and I met, Jack. That day? Only last year, but...

JACK. Of course, I remember.

BELLA. At the time, I felt so excited. *New*. It seemed that you *saw* me.

JACK. Yes. I did. A lonely princess.

BELLA. I was lonely. My parents were both gone so early, I'd been on my own for years, living in boarding schools, not really belonging to anyone. And do you remember, by the lake –

JACK. In Switzerland. Montreux, at dawn.

BELLA. Yes. I was standing there on the shore...

JACK. *(Crossing to her.)* You were all alone. You had a white dress and you had wrapped a blanket around yourself.

BELLA. I wanted to see the dawn. I was standing on the shore of that beautiful, still lake, watching the last traces of night leave the sky, feeling so lost...and I looked over toward the chalet and there you were –

JACK. *(Overlapping.)* There I was –

BELLA. – standing along the shoreline, looking at me.

JACK. Yes. I was waiting for you to see me. And then you did. Isn't that a happy memory?

BELLA. Yes, it is. I was so happy that we had found each other. And then to discover that we both were from England, from London even.

JACK. That we liked the same books and music...

BELLA. That we were both alone in the world. It was like a wonderful, romantic twist of Fate. But I don't know why we came back to England. Was it my idea? *(The question she has been working toward.)*

JACK. It was, yes. *(She knows this is not true.)*

BELLA. And to this house.

JACK. I suppose it was meant to be.

BELLA. "Meant to be." What does that mean? Is there such a thing as destiny, or...

JACK. Bella, what is this about? What –

BELLA. Let's leave here.

JACK. Pardon me?

BELLA. Let's leave this house, Jack. Let's find another home and start again! It was a mistake, I think, to live here. Once we learned what had happened.

JACK. Ah. Yes. I see what you mean. How long have you felt this way?

BELLA. I didn't want to say. I know you love this house. But I don't think I will be able to get better, living here. I'm sorry. I wish I were stronger.

JACK. Of course. I will look into it immediately.

BELLA. *(Astonished.)* Thank you.

JACK. *(Takes her in his arms.)* Your well-being is all I care about, Bella. If I were to lose you to – to this condition, it would only be because I have failed you. You are an angel to me.

Of course, we must leave this house. I only wish I had thought of it myself, before now.

> *(He rings the bell.)*

BELLA. *(In wonder.)* Jack – thank you. Thank you so much.

> **(ELIZABETH** *enters.)*

ELIZABETH. You rang, sir?

JACK. *(Holding* **BELLA***'s hand.)* Elizabeth, Mrs. Manningham and I have decided that we no longer wish to live in this house. Perhaps the ghosts of past events are contributing to Mrs. Manningham's ill feelings. We would very much appreciate it if you could assist us in readying ourselves and the house for a move, as soon as possible.

ELIZABETH. Oh!

JACK. Mrs. Manningham's health requires that we do so, and nothing is more important than that.

ELIZABETH. Of course, sir.

BELLA. I know this house has been your home for many years, Elizabeth. If you prefer to stay here, I'll understand. But I hope you'll consider coming with us.

ELIZABETH. Thank you, ma'am, that is most kind of you.

BELLA. Perhaps it's time for a fresh start for you, as well?

ELIZABETH. I – you may be right, ma'am.

JACK. Then it's decided – you'll come with us.

*(To **BELLA**.)* What do you say, my dear? A small Georgian terrace? Near a park, of course. Surely, we'll be able to find something cozy that we can afford.

BELLA. Oh, Jack! We'll be in heaven.

JACK. Yes.

Elizabeth, if you will help Mrs. Manningham to gather her things, I will make arrangements for the two of you to go immediately.

*(**JACK** is now at his desk, writing a note.)*

ELIZABETH. For the two of us, sir?

JACK. Well, yes. Until our new home can be found. I must stay here, to put things in order. There is much to be done! But, Elizabeth, Mrs. Manningham mustn't stay here a moment longer than is necessary.

(He seals the note and starts to exit.)

BELLA. You won't have breakfast, Jack?

JACK. I will. I'll just send this message and be back directly.

*(**JACK** exits.)*

ELIZABETH. Good heavens, ma'am!

BELLA. *(So happy.)* Yes. It is sudden, isn't it?

ELIZABETH. It is, but if you don't mind my saying so, I'm sure the change will do you good.

BELLA. You're right. I'm sure it will. And I'm so glad you are willing to come with us!

ELIZABETH. I should have gone, when it happened. I'm sure that I've dwelt too much on the past. Do you know, whenever I come into this room, I see the way it looked that night.

BELLA. It would not be easy to forget that sight.

ELIZABETH. I shouldn't speak of it.

BELLA. It's all right. It must have been awful. Was everything destroyed?

ELIZABETH. Oh, yes. The whole room torn to pieces, all her things attacked so furiously...

BELLA. How terrible. The killer was looking for the safe, I suppose.

ELIZABETH. Oh no, ma'am.

BELLA. But...

ELIZABETH. The safe was kept in the open. *(She indicates.)* It were right here. I don't see how anyone could have missed it.

BELLA. But then why destroy the room? What was he so angry about?

ELIZABETH. I'll confess, ma'am: I don't know. It was all very strange.

BELLA. What was?

ELIZABETH. Well, the whole story. About the safe. Miss Alice, she didn't keep things in there. Not jewelry. She never did, until that night.

BELLA. Oh.

ELIZABETH. She didn't believe in locking things away, where no one could enjoy them. "What's lovely is lovely, Elizabeth dear," she said. "It doesn't matter if it costs a million pounds or a shilling."

(**ELIZABETH** *rises to go.*)

I've always wondered why she locked them away that night. Perhaps she suspected that someone was coming to steal them.

BELLA. Perhaps she did. Or…

ELIZABETH. Or what, ma'am?

BELLA. Or everything was as usual, and the rubies weren't in the safe. The killer thought they would be, but they weren't.

ELIZABETH. I see. That's very clever, ma'am, if I may say so. I just thought what the police said must be right.

(*For a moment they are both lost in thought. Then* **ELIZABETH** *turns to the task at hand.*)

So we're to go on ahead, are we, Mrs.?

BELLA. (*Still thinking.*) Oh, yes. I suppose that is the plan.

ELIZABETH. Mr. Manningham will have a job of work to do, organizing everything on his own.

BELLA. Yes, I… (*A realization.*) He'll go through the whole house, won't he. Top to bottom. To make sure all is in order.

ELIZABETH. I would imagine so.

(*As* **BELLA** *looks around the room, a terrible understanding is taking hold.*)

How long will that take, do you think?

BELLA. (*Looking at her.*) I don't know.

(*They stand looking at each other, neither one ready to put her thoughts into words.*)

(**NANCY** *enters with breakfast.*)

ELIZABETH. What's that, then, miss? In the basket?

NANCY. It's muffins. The master had asked for them, so I went down the street and bought them. It were no trouble.

BELLA. Thank you, Nancy.

ELIZABETH. That'll be all, then. Off you go.

>   (**NANCY** *exits.*)

>   (*A slightly awkward moment, as neither* **BELLA** *nor* **ELIZABETH** *is sure what to do next. Then* **BELLA** *takes control.*)

BELLA. (*Quiet and calm.*) Elizabeth. In this room, is there anything else besides the portrait that belonged to Alice? The side tables, or the credenza?

ELIZABETH. Not the credenza, the letting agency put that here ma'am. Both the side tables were Miss Alice's though, and of course the portrait.

(*Cautiously.*) Is there anything else I can do for you, ma'am?

BELLA. I don't think so, Elizabeth. Thank you.

>   (**ELIZABETH** *exits.* **BELLA** *paces the room, calming herself. She hears the front door open and sits at the breakfast table again.*)

>   (**JACK** *enters.*)

JACK. Ah, delicious!

BELLA. (*Brightly.*) You've sent your message, have you?

JACK. Mm.

>   (*He sits down to eat.*)

BELLA. Jack, dear...

JACK. Yes?

BELLA. It's terribly kind of you to move houses just for me...for me and my – irrational –

JACK. Darling, it doesn't matter whether it is rational or not. If moving is what you need, that is what we shall do.

BELLA. I must still work at getting better though, mustn't I?

JACK. Of course. We must both –

BELLA. And I've been thinking about these things I do. Hiding things, moving things. Like that picture. I moved it again the other day, didn't I?

JACK. I'm afraid so. But I hope, as I know you do, that when we leave this house, your unfortunate delusions will –

BELLA. My delusions. Yes, that's right, that's what they are, I have delusions don't I.

JACK. I'm sorry Bella, but I think we should speak plainly. I don't mean to hurt you, dear.

BELLA. Yes. Thank you. I've been thinking about it so much, about my *delusions*, and I believe I've come to understand, at least a part of it.

JACK. And what's that?

BELLA. It's the portrait. I think I know why I've been moving that.

JACK. And why have you?

BELLA. Because of the rubies. *(This is what she has been driving toward.)*

JACK. The...?

BELLA. You must have heard Elizabeth mention them. The Barlow Rubies, they're quite famous. That's them, in the portrait.

JACK. Ah yes of course, I believe she has mentioned them.

BELLA. Such an extravagant gift. They were from an admirer, Elizabeth told me. A Prince, from somewhere in Eastern Europe or something like that.

JACK. How exotic.

BELLA. It was quite scandalous, apparently. These priceless jewels given by a young prince to a beautiful, unmarried, mature woman. Can you imagine all the gossip!

JACK. Indeed.

BELLA. They were worth – I don't know – thousands and thousands of pounds. And it was well known that Alice Barlow kept them here, in her house.

JACK. Did she.

BELLA. The killer must have come here looking for them. That's what Elizabeth said. So in the end, they caused her death. Such a tragedy, and for what?

JACK. Well, for the jewels. I would assume they're very beautiful. Intoxicating. Some men are seduced by that kind of thing. Gemstones are timeless, they seem to hold secrets thousands of years old, pulled from the depths of the earth, yet they glow as if... But you're right, of course. A tragic loss of life.

BELLA. Yes it was.

JACK. It's best not to become attached to the desire for a thing like that. If it gets its claws into you... A person might set out to own these jewels and find himself owned by them instead.

BELLA. Yes. I see how that might be. And I think that's why, sometimes, I don't want to look at those jewels, even in a painting.

JACK. Bella...

BELLA. They drove someone to murder. And Miss Barlow, she died for them.

JACK. Isn't that a bit melodramatic?

BELLA. Yes. You're right.

*(They eat their breakfast. **BELLA** continues, casually.)*

Do you know Jack, after all we've heard about them, I can't help wondering if those rubies might still be in the house somewhere.

JACK. What makes you say that?

BELLA. Well, the police didn't find them that night. Maybe the killer didn't find them, either.

JACK. Oh, that seems unlikely. They were taken from the safe, weren't they? Isn't that what Elizabeth said?

BELLA. Yes, she did, but...who knows?

JACK. Hmm.

BELLA. They could be in the attic, among Miss Alice's things.

JACK. Oh, surely not! They must be long gone. Sold to a wealthy collector.

BELLA. But wouldn't they have been discovered, by now?

JACK. I don't see why. These things are done in secret. Someone might pay an enormous sum for jewels like those, only to keep them locked away.

BELLA. But why?

JACK. To know that he has them in his power. And whoever had sold them would be...

BELLA. Rich beyond his dreams?

JACK. Yes. Or so I should think.

BELLA. You're right. That must be what happened. It would be silly to search through all of Alice Barlow's things on such a whim.

JACK. Yes. A bit silly. But that's all right.

BELLA. Especially the ones that are in the *attic* – the attic is so well sealed up.

JACK. Mm.

> (**BELLA** *drinks her tea.* **JACK** *looks up suddenly.*)

"The ones that are in the attic"?

BELLA. Yes, most of it is up there. Elizabeth moved it, and rented this other furniture when –

JACK. "Most of it"? Aren't all of her things up there?

BELLA. Well, yes. (*Looking around the room.*) Except the *credenza*, of course.

JACK. That was Alice Barlow's? I don't –

BELLA. Didn't you know? I suppose Elizabeth thought she may as well keep it there. It fits so well in that spot. And it would be very heavy to carry up the stairs.

It's a funny old piece, isn't it? So many locked drawers – a child's dream.

JACK. Where are the keys?

BELLA. All these secret places to hide your prized possessions. But Elizabeth says the keys were lost years ago.

JACK. Unh.

BELLA. They must be long gone, just like the rubies. I suppose we'll never know what happened to them.

Jack?

JACK. Yes, Bella.

BELLA. Your tea is getting cold.

Scene Four

*(Late that night. Darkness in the sitting room. We hear someone cautiously moving about – until he collides with a piece of furniture. Muffled cursing. We see **JACK**, with a small lantern, standing over the credenza. There is a wild and intense look in his eyes.)*

*(**JACK** takes out a knife, forces a drawer open. It's empty. He feels for a false bottom or hidden compartment, finds nothing. He moves on to another drawer, but it is stuck. Frustration building, he tries to force it, tries more violently, hurts his hand – now he can barely contain his pain and rage.)*

*(**ELIZABETH** enters with a light.)*

ELIZABETH. Oh, it's you, Mr. Manningham! I saw the light and...

JACK. Yes, just me, Elizabeth.

ELIZABETH. I'm sorry to disturb you, sir. I thought someone may be –

JACK. No, it's only me, I tripped in the dark.

ELIZABETH. I see, sir. Are you all right?

JACK. Just fine, thank you.

It's rather late, isn't it? But I don't seem able to sleep. I think I'll go out for a little stroll.

ELIZABETH. Yes, sir.

JACK. You can lock up behind me. I have my key.

ELIZABETH. Yes, sir.

(She follows him out of the room.)

(**BELLA** *steps out from behind the curtains.
She has heard everything. She stares at
the credenza for a moment and then her
shoulders sag as she begins to cry.*)

Scene Five

(Late in the evening, a few days later.)

*(**BELLA** stands in the drawing room, perfectly still. We get the impression that she has been there for a while. Above, the dragging and shuffling sounds. She listens. The gaslight is dim. A repeat of what we saw in Act One, except for the effect this has on **BELLA**. She waits, detached.)*

*(Finally, the noises stop. The gaslight goes up. **BELLA** moves to the sofa, deals out a game of solitaire and composes herself. A few moments later, **JACK** enters. He is surprised to see **BELLA**. She is not surprised to see him.)*

BELLA. Oh! Jack. You startled me. I didn't expect you home yet. Is anything the matter?

JACK. Not at all. I finished early at the club and I thought I might do some work here before bed. I'm surprised to see you still up. Aren't you tired?

BELLA. Yes, but I couldn't sleep.

JACK. Would you like a drink? Sherry?

BELLA. No, thank you.

JACK. I believe I will have one.

So this is what you do in the evenings when I am hard at work entertaining clients?

BELLA. Who were you entertaining?

JACK. What?

BELLA. Who were you meeting?

JACK. No one you know, Bella. I wanted to see if I could –
One has to build a network. What did you think I was
doing?

BELLA. Oh, I wouldn't know, of course. I really don't
understand such things.

> (**BELLA** *has finished or abandoned her game,
> she shuffles the deck for another.*)

JACK. No.

Let's have a game of Beggar.

> (*He splits the deck between them.*)

Do you think this is what other married couples do in
the evenings?

BELLA. I don't –

JACK. (*He plays a card, chuckles.*) Beggar, my dear!

BELLA. (*Watching him as he picks up the pile of cards.*)
Jack?

JACK. Yes, dear.

BELLA. About our plans. The move. I'm not sure – I worry
a bit about your being all alone here.

JACK. Why should that worry you?

BELLA. What will you do?

JACK. Well, I'll be busy –

BELLA. You and Nancy, I mean.

JACK. I will be very busy arranging to move our household.

BELLA. But you don't need to live here to do that, do you?

JACK. It's more convenient. What is this really about?

BELLA. I was just thinking...for appearances...

JACK. Are you saying you're worried there might be gossip about our marriage?

BELLA. It might seem ridiculous to you, dear, but with you and Nancy here alone... I only want to protect you. You know how people can be.

JACK. Are you suggesting –

BELLA. There you are, alone in the house with an attractive maid while your wife is... I hate that we to have to think this way, but – what will people say?

JACK. Don't be ridiculous. No one could think that, after I have been so obviously –

BELLA. But what if they do? If people think there is something unsavory going on, they'll watch this house like hawks. You don't want to come under scrutiny, dear, do you?

JACK. Bella, I'm sure...

BELLA. No. I can't let you be *exposed* that way. We should keep things the way they are. Our quiet life that no one notices. Yes. Elizabeth and I will stay here with you until all the business is concluded.

JACK. That's very kind of you. But are you sure...?

BELLA. That I can survive a few more weeks here? Yes. Knowing you need me will give me the strength.

JACK. You're very brave, my dear.

BELLA. *(Sweetly.)* Your love gives me the courage.

And the more I know about what you need to do, the more I can help you.

JACK. It's just the usual: making arrangements, getting the place ready to be let again. We must leave it as we found it, you know.

BELLA. I suppose you'll have to go up into the attic – go through Miss Alice's things.

JACK. The attic? Why?

BELLA. To check for damage. Remember, Elizabeth said the roof may have leaked during those summer storms. We can't let mildew set in. Don't worry, I'll help you with it. When should we begin?

JACK. This is a sudden change of heart.

BELLA. Perhaps. But –

JACK. Oh, most certainly it is. I'm sorry to say that it's a bit alarming.

BELLA. Why?

JACK. Your moods, Bella, have become more and more erratic. Just a few days ago you couldn't bear to live here a moment longer. You were so traumatized by the sight of that portrait that by your own admission you were compelled to move it, in a trancelike state, over and over again. I'm sorry, but this sudden decision to stay can only be another example of irrational behaviour.

BELLA. But I'm not –

JACK. I am an extremely patient man. I think I have demonstrated this, but there comes a point...

BELLA. "...there comes a point"?

JACK. A few days ago, I contacted a doctor who has experience in matters of the mind.

BELLA. Why would you –

JACK. On my request, he is ready to make a house call at any time. And I assure you that I will follow his expert advice. Should that be necessary. Is it necessary now, Bella?

BELLA. No. I –

JACK. Good. But if it is, if you need some time away, where your treatment can be properly administered –

BELLA. I don't need – Jack – *you know that I don't need –*

JACK. I do not know that. Bella, from one day to the next I don't know what I will encounter from you. This evening, in fact, I return home to find my overwrought wife playing cards in the middle of the night, for no explicable reason.

BELLA. I'm only –

JACK. The staff can attest to your erratic behaviour – if you think they haven't observed it, you are very mistaken.

BELLA. The staff...

JACK. Of course. Aside from everything else, you accused them of theft. The more you protest, the more you prove our point. You simply aren't rational, my dear.

BELLA. Jack –

JACK. Don't worry. When the time comes – if and when your actions make it necessary – the doctor will know what to do.

I won't let you down. I owe it to you, my one and only Bella, to take the best possible care. After all, if I allowed this behaviour to go on...what would people say?

Good night my dear. Don't stay up all night.

(He kisses her lightly and leaves.)

*(***BELLA*** watches him leave and, after a desperate look around, buries her head in her hands.)*

Scene Six

(The next evening. **JACK** *and* **ELIZABETH**.*)*

JACK. It was last night. She was sleepwalking, or else in a trance of some kind. I found her standing here, staring up at this portrait. In fact, when I came in, Mrs. Manningham was in the act of removing the portrait from the wall again.

ELIZABETH. Oh! Oh dear, sir!

JACK. She won't remember doing it, of course.

ELIZABETH. So it is becoming...

JACK. Yes. You know where all this leads.

ELIZABETH. Yes.

JACK. I think you've heard that Mrs. Manningham's mother never returned from the mad house. Very tragic.

ELIZABETH. Yes.

JACK. Thank you, Elizabeth. Your assistance is greatly appreciated.

ELIZABETH. Yes, sir. I only want to help, sir.

JACK. I know you do. The doctor's men will be coming soon. Tonight, in fact. Quite late.

ELIZABETH. In the night, sir!

JACK. Yes. It is best done in the small hours, to avoid gossip. What would people say? I hope we can persuade Mrs. Manningham to go with them calmly.

ELIZABETH. Yes, sir.

JACK. I'll have to spend some time on the house then. The estate managers agree that it would be best to do some redecorating. I will see to it.

ELIZABETH. Ah.

JACK. Once the work begins it's difficult to say how far we may have to go. I hope we won't have to remove too many walls or floorboards due to the damp. Of course, that has been a problem all over as of late.

ELIZABETH. Yes, sir.

JACK. Mrs. Manningham has confided in you, hasn't she? About her delusions. She *has* spoken of it?

ELIZABETH. Yes sir. She has, sir.

JACK. Good, then. You won't have any difficulty repeating that information for the doctor. As well as telling what you yourself have seen.

ELIZABETH. I'll help in any way I can.

JACK. Very good. Thank you, Elizabeth. It is difficult for all of us. But I will see that you are properly compensated, once it's all over.

ELIZABETH. Yes sir.

JACK. Just continue on as you have been, for the rest of this evening. Don't give out that anything unusual is happening.

> (**JACK** *picks up his hat and stick.*)

ELIZABETH. Good evening, sir.

> (**JACK** *exits. A moment later,* **NANCY** *enters somewhat furtively. She stops, startled, on seeing* **ELIZABETH.***)

Well? What brings you in here? I don't recall as the master or missus called for you.

NANCY. No, missus. I thought I had left my – my gloves in here.

ELIZABETH. Well, you haven't. But so long as you're here, you may as well clean the fireplace grate. Mind you don't get ashes on the rug.

NANCY. But it's –

ELIZABETH. It's only half six o'clock, missy. Had plans for yourself, did you?

NANCY. No.

> (**ELIZABETH** *exits.* **NANCY** *crosses to the desk. She sits in Jack's chair and runs her fingers over the desktop.*)

> (**BELLA** *enters.*)

> (**NANCY** *leaps out of the desk chair.*)

Good evening, ma'am.

BELLA. Good evening, Nancy. Is there something you wanted here?

NANCY. No ma'am. I just meant to –

BELLA. Yes?

NANCY. My gloves, I – thought they were...

BELLA. *Gloves.* I see. Well. They don't appear to be on Mr. Manningham's desk.

> (**NANCY** *moves farther from the desk. The gaslight goes down.* **BELLA** *notices it.*)

NANCY. No, ma'am. If you'll excuse me, I'll just...

> (*Above, the sounds begin.* **NANCY** *and* **BELLA** *stare at one another.* **NANCY** *begins to exit.*)

BELLA. Nancy.

NANCY. Yes, ma'am.

BELLA. Do you hear that? That noise, overhead?

> (**NANCY** *considers her options.*)

NANCY. Noise, ma'am?

BELLA. Yes. Surely you can...

NANCY. Oh yes. Those noises you thought you were hearing. I've heard you speakin' to Elizabeth about it. But Elizabeth hasn't heard them and neither have I. It must be your imagination, ma'am.

BELLA. I see.

NANCY. May I go now, ma'am?

BELLA. No. Please don't.

NANCY. Is there something else?

BELLA. Yes there is, but I'm not sure – I suppose I should start by asking you what my husband has promised you.

NANCY. Promised me, ma'am?

BELLA. Please. It's not worth denying. You've heard him up in the attic, you can hear him right now. We both can. But why are you lying about it?

NANCY. What makes you think –

BELLA. It's Jack, you know it as well as I do. He's up there searching, as he has almost every night since we've lived in this house.

NANCY. Searching for [what?] –

BELLA. And if you know he's there, you must know what he's after.

NANCY. How would I –

BELLA. It's the rubies, isn't it? Alice Barlow's rubies. Never mind; of course it is. Nancy, do you understand that the rubies are *all that he wants*? Once he has them, he'll –

NANCY. He'll what?

BELLA. He won't need you anymore. Do you understand?

NANCY. I don't –

BELLA. Listen to me. I really believe you're in danger. Look, I can prove it – let me show you –

> (**BELLA** *picks up the letter opener and opens the drawer, this time breaking the lock in her haste. The pearl necklace is gone.*)

My pearls. They were here – I swear it. You remember – the ones I searched for, the ones you were accused of stealing. They were here in his drawer all along. Don't you see, that means –

> (**NANCY** *laughs out loud.*)

(*Realizing.*) You knew. Nancy. You knew what he was doing to me, all along.

Listen. Whatever Jack has promised you, when he finds the rubies, he'll –

NANCY. He'll never find them.

BELLA. *What do you know about this?*

NANCY. I know he's a fool. Almost as big a fool as you are.

> (*Another noise, right above them.*)

Yes, it's him. He makes noise in the attic, he hides your things and blames it on you, he's persuaded you – and Elizabeth too, I suppose – that you're weak in the head. I'm only surprised it took you this long to see it.

BELLA. But if you –

NANCY. Look at you, shaking like a leaf. First you loved him, now you're afraid of him.

BELLA. You should be too. You've been helping him, but –

NANCY. Of course I have. I know a lucky chance when I see one. That's his way into the attic: through my bedroom window.

BELLA. But why –

NANCY. He told me the whole story. How Alice Barlow was his friend, she promised the rubies to him –

BELLA. He's lying! Can't you see –

NANCY. Well, of course he is! Anyone can see that.

BELLA. Then why...?

NANCY. Oh, I can't bear it anymore, watching you carry on over him. Whatever happens to you, it's your own fault. You wanted him to save you. Why didn't you save yourself?

And now it's too late. Jack will have you taken away. Can't you see how he's outsmarted you?

BELLA. It doesn't have to –

NANCY. What will you say to them? "My husband had my necklace in his desk." "My husband got into the attic."

BELLA. I know that. It's my word against his. But if you know he's lying about Alice, why are you – *(Realizing.)* Oh.

NANCY. I've got all I needed from him. He's not going to find any rubies in the attic. He's been searching all this time. But he's thinking about it wrong. *(The portrait.)* Look at her. Anyone can see it. *She* liked to make a show. She's not the type to stuff jewels inside old furniture. She could have put them anywhere, or somewhere queer, for a joke, like. As soon as you are locked away –

BELLA. Nancy, please.

> *(The gaslight comes up, but neither of them notices it.)*

It's not too late. Yes, I've been a fool, but so have you. If you'll help me –

NANCY. No! I've been waiting for this. This is my chance, finally. You'll be taken away tonight, while I'm out. *I'll* find the rubies, while Jack skulks in the attic tearing up upholstery. And then I'll be gone, and I'll never be anyone's servant again, not ever.

BELLA. But can't you see how much danger you are in? Think about it. If Jack knows the killer didn't find the rubies, it's because he was there that night. Nancy, *Jack is the killer.*

NANCY. I don't –

BELLA. You *should* care. What will happen if he finds them before you do? Do you really think he wants to share them with you?

NANCY. I –

BELLA. *(Shushes **NANCY**.)* When did that happen? He's coming. Quickly – look, the light has gone up, that means he's coming back. He'll be here any moment. He can't know we've been talking about – Nancy!

> *(But **NANCY** is gone. **BELLA** hurriedly shuts Jack's broken desk drawer. **JACK** enters.)*

JACK. Hello, dear. Are you all right?

BELLA. Oh yes – yes, thank you. You're back so early!

JACK. Did you want me to stay away longer?

BELLA. Oh no, I – I'm surprised to see you, that's all.

JACK. Was that Nancy I saw, just now?

BELLA. Yes, it must have been.

JACK. Is something wrong?

BELLA. I just sent her on an errand, to the kitchen.

JACK. Ah. Well, as it happens, I'm not back early, not really. I forgot something.

BELLA. Oh, I see.

> (**JACK** *crosses to the desk.* **BELLA** *holds her breath. He unlocks a drawer, not the one* **BELLA** *had opened.*)

JACK. In a hurry to be rid of me, are you?

BELLA. Of course not. It's a shame that you have to work so much in the evenings.

JACK. Tonight I won't be long.

> (**JACK** *has removed some papers from the drawer. He re-locks it, then looks more closely at* **BELLA**.)

Bella.

BELLA. Yes?

JACK. What were you and Nancy talking about?

BELLA. Nothing, I –

JACK. It's no use lying to me.

BELLA. Why would I?

JACK. I don't know. Why would you? Let's ask Nancy to come in here.

BELLA. All right.

> (*She crosses to the call bell, puts a hand out, hesitates.*)

JACK. Go ahead. Call for her.

> (**BELLA** *pulls the bell. They wait.*)

Are you sure you can't remember?

BELLA. I – it was nothing. We...

(The lamp – the one with the beaded trim on its shade – is between them. BELLA's eye falls on it and she realizes something. JACK's gaze sharpens.)

JACK. What is it?

BELLA. What? Yes, Jack?

JACK. I said, "What is it," Bella. You look like you have seen a ghost.

(He notices the letter opener and picks it up.)

*(**JACK** crosses quickly toward **BELLA**; she shrinks back. He smiles slightly, then reaches past her to pull the call bell again.)*

Where has she gotten to?

BELLA. This might be her evening out. I'm afraid I haven't kept track of those things very well.

JACK. Bella, you had better tell me why you were so startled when I came in.

(He holds the letter opener in what could be a threatening way.)

BELLA. I'm sorry. *(Thinking fast.)* To be honest, Jack... I was frightened again tonight.

JACK. Again!

BELLA. I know. I told you I wouldn't be. I thought I wouldn't. And then I was. I called Nancy in here to – well, for company, I suppose. I asked her to sit with me, but she didn't want to. I should have told you the truth. I just... I wanted you to think I was getting better.

JACK. I see. Well, don't worry, dear. We'll have it all sorted out soon.

> *(He puts the letter opener down on the desk and picks up the papers.)*

I'll be back shortly.

BELLA. And I'll...rest.

JACK. That's a good idea. *(He kisses her on the forehead.)* Rest.

> *(**JACK** exits. **BELLA** violently wipes his kiss from her forehead, then turns back into the room with new determination.)*

Scene Seven

(A few hours later. Darkness outside. **BELLA** *sits quietly, waiting. The letter opener is no longer on the desk.)*

*(***JACK*** *enters, surprised to see her there.)*

JACK. Hello. Still up?

BELLA. I didn't feel tired, after all.

JACK. Ah.

(Pause while he pours himself a drink, checks his pocket watch.)

BELLA. Are you expecting someone?

JACK. Of course not. Not at this hour. Were you waiting up for me?

BELLA. Yes.

JACK. Ah.

(He drinks his drink and stands with the empty glass, watching her.)

Is there something on your mind?

BELLA. Well, yes. I thought we should... I'm afraid you were right, Jack.

JACK. Was I.

BELLA. Yes. Living in this house, it's too much for me. It was a mistake to think I could stay here with you.

JACK. Don't worry about that.

BELLA. Elizabeth and I should go on ahead, as you planned.

JACK. Mmm.

BELLA. *(Looking around.)* It's a shame, though. It will be hard to find another place to let so cheaply, won't it?

JACK. It could be.

BELLA. The history of this place...that must discourage people.

What a tragedy. It doesn't seem worth it.

JACK. Worth what?

BELLA. Those jewels. The Barlow Rubies.

JACK. Oh.

BELLA. I've thought of them often, this last while. Do you think they're worth it?

JACK. Bella, how would I even –

BELLA. I don't.

> *(Beat.)*

Poor Elizabeth. I really think it weighs on her.

JACK. *(Possibly a bit exasperated.) What* does, my dear?

BELLA. The murder. She feels guilty. She didn't hear anything that night, you know.

JACK. Oh.

BELLA. She didn't hear Alice being killed. They found her on the floor, here, remember? I told you. And the safe was forced open. That's why they thought the rubies were stolen.

JACK. Mm...

> *(Beat.)*

They *"thought"* –?

BELLA. Yes. But, of course, they were wrong about that. That's where the police made their mistake. Here's what I think: the rubies weren't stolen that night at all, because the killer looked for them in the safe. And they weren't *in* the safe.

Were they.

(*Everything stops.*)

JACK. Excuse me?

BELLA. The killer opened the safe, and the rubies weren't there. But by then the neighbours were awake, police had been sent for. You know, because of the screaming. Alice. So, he had to run away, and leave the rubies behind. Somewhere in the house.

Right?

(*Softly.*) You must have been angry, when there wasn't time to look for them.

JACK. Bella, what do you...

BELLA. Do you know, since I learned the truth about us, I've been asking myself, *why*? Once I realized that you were hiding my things, and your own, that you took down the picture from the wall, and told me I was losing my senses...and all those other things...

JACK. Are you sure you want to –

BELLA. At first, I thought you just enjoyed being cruel. But it was more...*practical*, wasn't it? You wanted me here. In this house. Here, but not – capable. You wanted a wife who would trust you more than she trusted herself. But still, I thought, *why*?

JACK. I don't know where you –

BELLA. And then, finally, when I realized the Barlow Rubies may not have been stolen at all – *yet* –

JACK. Bella, this is really – your behaviour is –

BELLA. Is what, Jack? Irrational? Paranoid?

JACK. Perhaps you should –

BELLA. But wouldn't you like to *know*?

JACK. Know what?

BELLA. If you keep interrupting me, you'll never find out where they are.

> *(A pause.* **JACK** *and* **BELLA** *stare each other down. Finally, he sits, watching her.)*

It was all a lie, from the beginning. Every single moment of our relationship has been a lie.

You had to get back into this house. You knew the rubies were here, somewhere. But you had already spent what little you got in the robbery, and you had nothing else. Then you saw your chance. Me, all alone, with no one to care for me but with a little bit of money – just enough to get you back to England and to let this house.

JACK. Where are they, Bella?

BELLA. It wasn't enough to get here. You needed *me* here too. You'd be too noticeable, rattling around here by yourself. Neighbours would be curious. I was the perfect excuse. The devoted husband, so worried about his poor mad wife.

JACK. If you'd only –

BELLA. So you kept me on the edge. And once you had the rubies, you would give that final push. Over the brink. I'd be locked up somewhere, and you would go back to being – whoever you were before.

JACK. Bella, I –

BELLA. *Don't*. Of course it was you. You killed Alice, and *then* you realized you needed her. Because only Alice knew where they were.

JACK. Alice and *you*.

BELLA. Well, yes. But not until tonight. In fact it was Elizabeth who knew they must be here, though she didn't realize she knew it.

And then – Nancy. Really, Jack...

(*Off* **JACK***'s reaction:*) She saw through you long before I did, you know. But I expect she's clever enough to be gone for good.

It was Nancy who showed me what we had all missed: that a woman like Alice Barlow, of such vitality, with such a mischievous sense of humour... well, if there's one place she would not have put those rubies, it's...out of sight.

> (**BELLA** *is standing by the table lamp. For the first time we, and* **JACK***, notice something different about it. It looks plainer, now. It is missing its slightly gaudy beaded trim.* **JACK***'s face grows pale.*)

JACK. No. No no no no...

BELLA. Yes. Right under your handsome, aquiline nose. Every day.

But not anymore.

JACK. (*Quietly pulling the desk drawer open.*) Where are they now. Where?

> (**JACK** *pulls the gun from the drawer, aims it at* **BELLA**.*)*

So, you forced open my desk drawer. You should have taken the gun. Don't make the mistake of thinking that I wouldn't shoot you.

BELLA. I would never think that. But would you really kill the only person who can tell you where they are?

JACK. Of course not. I'll just shoot you in the kneecap.

    (He checks the gun, shakes his head.)

You didn't even unload it. Are you sure you won't tell me?

BELLA. Quite sure.

JACK. That's a shame. I don't really want to hurt you – though I've been tempted, a few times. You're right, of course I tricked you. It was disappointingly easy. But I did regret, sometimes, having to put us both through all that. I even...yes: I did feel sorry for you, sometimes.

BELLA. Did you.

JACK. Still, it's the strong that survive, and you weren't.

    (He pulls back the hammer.)

And now you tell me where they are.

BELLA. I don't think so.

        *(**JACK** pulls the trigger. Nothing happens. He pulls it again and again.)*

I can't blame you for underestimating me. I was such a fool. But not fool enough to find your gun and leave the firing pin in place.

        *(**JACK** lunges for **BELLA**. She evades him; he chases her. Furniture is overturned. She pulls out the letter opener, but he gets it from her. He has her by the throat, choking her.)*

JACK. *Where – are – they?* TELL. ME. TELL. ME.

        *(**JACK** raises the letter opener. The door bursts open. **ELIZABETH** enters with a cast-iron skillet. She cracks **JACK** over the head and he crumples to the floor.)*

Scene Eight

(A few minutes later. **JACK** *is tied to a chair.
His head lolls.* **BELLA** *and* **ELIZABETH** *stand
looking at him.)*

BELLA. Do you think it will hold?

ELIZABETH. Oh, I should think so, Mrs... Miss Bella.

BELLA. I thought you were going to use the coal scuttle.

ELIZABETH. Yes. But in the end I decided the skillet were
heavier. *(She hefts it.)* And easier to handle.

(They regard him for a moment.)

I always knew he was a bad one.

BELLA. Did you?

ELIZABETH. Dear me, yes! Asking me to speak to the doctor,
to tell him you weren't right in your head? Always telling
you to rest.

BELLA. Thank you, Elizabeth.

ELIZABETH. Rest from *him*, that's what you needed.

*(***JACK*** begins to stir. Groggily, he realizes he
is tied up.)*

BELLA. Could you make us some tea? You and me, that is.

ELIZABETH. That I will.

*(***ELIZABETH*** glowers at* **JACK** *again and exits.)*

JACK. Bella – Bella.

BELLA. Yes, Jack?

JACK. Please – let me explain – come closer.

(She crosses to him.)

BELLA. What is it?

JACK. These ropes – they're so tight. I can't feel my hands, I –

BELLA. *(Checking the ropes.)* It's no use. Those are good knots. Elizabeth grew up in a fishing village, you know.

JACK. *(He leans his head against hers.)* Bella. I'm sorry. I'm sorry, darling – I lied to you – I should have trusted you. I should have told you everything.

BELLA. *(Softly.)* Why didn't you?

JACK. I don't know, I thought...it was a mistake.

BELLA. Yes. I am your wife.

JACK. Yes! And I should have realized from the start – how clever you are.

BELLA. It's true, I am.

JACK. You solved the mystery.

BELLA. I did.

JACK. And you have them. The rubies.

BELLA. I do.

JACK. Show them to me! I have it all arranged – a buyer. He's been waiting. Come with me! Do you know how much money we'll have, my darling? We'll never have to worry about our fortune again. We can be together, go anywhere you like. Back to Switzerland! Wherever you choose, my love! Just untie me, quickly, or cut the ropes, there are scissors in my desk, you can

*(**BELLA** crosses to the desk, opens drawers.)*

Yes, there – get the scissors, Bella. We'll –

BELLA. *(At the desk.)* Oh look, Jack. Here's the grocery bill. Remember, the one you were asking me for. I thought I'd lost it.

JACK. I don't – it must've –

BELLA. Oh, and here's the key to my work box. I was looking for that the other day.

JACK. Bella...are you going to...

BELLA. *(Rummaging around a bit.)* But do you know what I wish were here, what I really wish I could find again... is my pearl necklace. My mother's pearls.

You gave them to Nancy, didn't you?

JACK. I – no, I...

BELLA. I wish you hadn't done that, Jack.

JACK. Bella!

BELLA. I'm sorry. I've gotten distracted. Here are the scissors. *(Sighs.)* If only I weren't *irrational*. If I had my wits about me, I might be able to take these scissors and cut the ropes.

It's a shame, really. Your poor mad wife.

What I should do now is *rest*, shouldn't I. Isn't that what you usually suggest, Jack?

> *(**JACK** groans.)*

> *(Sound of voices out in the street and a carriage pulling up. **BELLA** goes to the window.)*

Ah: here they are. I suppose there isn't time for a rest, just now.

JACK. No – you didn't –

BELLA. No, I didn't. *You* did, remember? You arranged for people to come, tonight, and take me away. You must have thought I was about to guess the truth.

JACK. *(Continuing to struggle.)* Bella, please!

BELLA. They'll find this overturned furniture, and Elizabeth will tell how you attacked me.

> *(She shows him the bruise forming at her throat.)*

And then there's whatever mess you've made up in the attic... Did you think I didn't know?

Every night, when you turned up the gaslight in the attic, the light in the rest of the house went down just a bit. I can see by your face that you did not know that. It was very frightening, at first.

JACK. Bella – let me see them...just once, let me...

> *(He lets out a cry of rage and frustration.)*

BELLA. Yes! I feel the same way. That pain you feel over the rubies – I felt it over you. You were everything to me, Jack. But you loved *them*. And you will never, ever see them.

> *(She suddenly kneels at his feet, staring up into his face.)*

Can't you see? It was *me*, Jack. *I* was your jewel. Don't you remember, in Proverbs:

"Who can find a virtuous woman? For her price is far above rubies. She will do him good and not evil all the days of her life."

And I would have.

End of Play